Dogscrimination

Is Rampant Across Our Nation

Dogscrimination

Is Rampant Across Our Nation

By

Jafra

Dedication

This book is dedicated to all of the animals in the world; from the loved and pampered to the neglected, abused and oppressed.

Contents

Introduction

Laramie is a beautiful Bichon Frise' who lives with her human parents, Genie and Ken, as well as an older brother, a black and grey tabby cat, named Floyd.

Bichon Frise' is French for curly lap dog. They are petite, sturdy dogs with curly white fur, a black nose and dark round eyes. They are naturally

Jafra

happy dogs who are inquisitive, intelligent, playful and affectionate. They are genuinely sociable dogs. They are zealous for the company of humans and cannot be home alone for exceedingly long stretches of time. They thrive on companionship.

Although her humans primarily worked out of their home, Laramie simply wasn't satisfied with the amount of time she was with her humans.

Chapter One

An Ordinary Day

Murrff.

Nothing.

Mmuurrff.

Still nothing.

Mmmuuurrrfff, sniffs out.

Lying on her side and not moving, Genie sleepily says mmm.

Jafra

Ummmmuuuurrrrffff, errrrrrrrr, sniffs out and stomps her front right paw.

Mmm, give me *five* more minutes.

With both front paws, she pushes on Genie's shoulders. Get up lazy bones. Get up!

Okay, okay. Stomp your foot again.

Stomp!

Ha, ha, ha! Laramie, you're like a stuffed animal with a pulse. You are so smart, funny *and* sweet. Good morning feng shweet.

Mama, that's not right. It's feng shui which has nothing to do with me. It has something to do with decorating.

It's a play on words, feng shweet. She proceeded to sing a silly ditty she made up about Laramie:

> *I'mmmmm feng shweet*
> *I'm schweet as a day dream*
> *I'm shweeter than ice cream*

Dogscrimination

On a hottt, sunny day

Fennnggg shweet

I'm shweet as a rainbow

I'm shweet as Tim Teeeeebow

Onnn the fooootball field

They both giggle.

I love you Laramie!

Yeah, I love you too. It's 'cause we're best friends and all. It's funny, you're my best friend, I'm your best friend, we know each other and we live at the same place! You've been my best friend practically my whole life. Have I been your best friend your whole life Mama?

No feng shweet, I'm a *little* bit older than you. She rolls out of bed and slips on her clogs.

Laramie stands up on her back legs, Genie hugs her and then says beep, beep, beep, beep, beep, as she lifts Laramie up in the air and puts her down.

Let's go get the paper.

Okay Mama.

Side by side they trip down the hallway, down the stairs and out the front door. Genie gets the paper while Laramie does her "business".

With the newspaper in one hand, Genie hunches over, waves her arms over her head, curls up her fingers on the other hand, makes an **arrrrwwwww** monster-growl, while chasing Laramie back into the house, up the stairs and into the kitchen. They both giggle.

Laramie, would you like some C-O-T-T-A-G-E C-H-E-E-S-E?

Laramie stands on her back legs and with her front paws, she and her mom double high-five.

Yes, oh, yes, that would be delightful. Cottage cheese makes me happy!

Cottage cheese makes me happy too. Singing, to the tune of "The Mickey Mouse Club March" by Jimmie Dodd, C-O-T-T-A-G-E C-H-E-E-S-E and shouts cottage cheese, cottage cheese, cottage cheese, as she puts a spoonful in Laramie's bowl. Laramie, talking while eating, mmm, yum, oh, this is so good, thank you.

My pleasure. She pours a cup of coffee and sits at the breakfast nook to read the paper.

Laramie gallivants into the living room to play but is distracted by kids walking down the street. She rushes to the window, bark, bark, bark, bark, bark, erruff!

It's the neighbor kids walking to school, feng shweet.

She gallops to her basket of toys. Where is that green mouse? Ah, there you are. Hi Ira! She runs back to the living room, flops down, stretches out and rolls over onto her back. She begins tossing

Ira up and down in the air while singing to the tune of "The Bridge on the River Kwai" theme song by Malcolm Arnold:

Ira

The Irish green furred mouse

Ira

The mouse without a house

Ira

Oh, oh, oh Ira

Oh, oh, oh Ira

The green furred mouse

She tosses Ira aside, leaps onto the sofa and starts playing with the cushions. Arrrrr, arrrr, arrrr, arrrr, as she boisterously slides under the pillows, tossing them in the air and one by one landing on the floor. Plop, plop, plop. She drags the throw off the sofa and chuckles while rolling herself up in it. She rolls out of the throw, jumps up, shakes her whole body and looks around the room for something else to do. She vaults to the chair that houses the daily newspapers of the past week. She crumples them up and when she springs off the chair, all of the papers fall to the floor. She jets off to see what's in the trash can in the master bathroom. She plucks out a soap wrapper and then an empty toothpaste carton. She finds a tissue with lipstick on it and puts it under the bed. She returns to the trash can to pull out cough lozenge wrappers, gum wrappers and an empty cotton ball bag. She scampers to her toy basket, pulls out a baby bunny and goes into her mom's closet to aptly place the bunny in one of her mom's shoes.

Ken walks in the living room, **Laramie**!

She tiptoes in with her head hanging down and her round, cocoa-colored eyes sheepishly peering up through her fur at her dad.

Young lady, you have made a shambles of this room. I'll bet you've been in the trash can too.

Uh, yeah, but I, uh, I'm looking out for you and Mom. Iya, um, check the trash can to make sure you haven't thrown anything good away.

Floyd saunters through the living room and says Laramie, you are a mess in a dress sister. Ha, you amaze me the shenanigans you're constantly getting into.

Listen, playing is one of my favorite things to do. In fact, I am behind on my play and I have much to do today.

As he slinks to exit, he says perhaps but you have a counterproductive propensity to transmogrify an exceptionally immaculate room to one that appears as if a vehement tornado devastated it.

Dogscrimination

She says ho hum and yawns. She watches her dad clean up the disaster area she created from her antics.

While gathering up the newspapers, he notices the movie guide. He calls out, Genie.

Yes.

Let's go see a movie later.

Sounds like a plan!

Dogscrimination

Chapter Two

I'll Run Away

Laramie, why are you crying?

Floydy boy, I heard Mom and Dad say they are   going to the movies, **AGAIN**. I'll be home alone, **AGAIN.**

I perceive crying about this episode to be irrational. I am at the height of tranquility when they're absent.

Jafra

I *want* to be with them. I am not like you. I need them.

Oh, it slipped my mind, that's one of the innumerable gaps betwixt the emotional intelligence of cats and dogs. Cats don't miss the humans and dogs pine away at their truancy. Regardless, dogs can't go everyplace humans go so that's why you're home alone sometimes.

It's not right! I like to explore new places and I am not allowed to because I'm a dog. They go to the movies, I can't go. They go to the fitness center, I can't go. The fitness center has kid fit and I don't understand why there's not *dog* fit 'cause dogs are just as important as stinky, sticky kids! I can't go to the grocery store, restaurants or the library. Why? NO DOGS ALLOWED, that's why! Argh, it makes me mad, M-A-D, mad!

Laramie, it's discrimination.

Disrimnation?

Dogscrimination

No, discrimination.

What's that?

It's the unfair treatment of a person or group because of some form of prejudice.

Human beans deem themselves superior? I don't understand how human beans can be so egocentric sometimes.

Human what?

Beans.

It's human *beings* not beans.

Reeeeally?

Yes.

Whew, what a relief! I mean, human beans eating beans seems cannibalistic. Anyhow, I still don't grasp why they hold themselves supreme.

Laramie, not only is it complicated, I think you might be too young to comprehend. I have to go. Arrivederci.

Ciao Floydy boy.

Laramie goes to her bed and continues crying. She thought *they're going to the movies without me and it's da, di, dos,* **dogscrimination.** *Don't they realize how important I am? Well, I'll show them. I'll run away from home. Boy, oh boy, will that ever show 'em!*

She hastens to the door, whines and her human, Genie, lets her out. Laramie wriggles through the gate and gets out of the fenced back yard. With great confidence and immeasurable self-esteem, she scoots down the street with her white fluffy tail arched over her back. It's waving to and fro like a national flag. Her ears are bopping up and down with each step taken. She sees her best friend CoCo, a brown miniature dachshund, outside playing.

Hi CoCo!

Hey Laramie, what's going on?

I'm running away from home.

What? Why?

My parents are going to see a movie and I don't get to go.

Is that all? My humans go places without me all the time. In fact, I'm home alone for a couple of days.

Well, it's dogscrimination and I'm protesting by running away from home.

Dog what?

Dogscrimination. It's the unfair treatment of dogs. I'm tired of dogscrimination. They go to the fitness center without me, the movie theatre, grocery store, concerts, vacations, high and low, here and there without me. CoCo, let's face it, dogscrimination is rampant across our nation!

Aw Laramie, you're being melodramatic, girlfriend. Hang out with me while my humans are gone and we'll have F-U-N, fun, fun, fun!

Jafra

Laramie pushes her front paws in the air and says woop woop, coolio, let's go.

They set out for a lengthy excursion in their neighborhood. First, they went to Laramie's Uncle Daniel's house. His trash can was at the end of his driveway awaiting pick up. Laramie stood up on her back legs, CoCo climbed onto her shoulders and stood up on her back legs. She could barely reach the top of the trash can with her front paws but managed to tip it over. They proceeded strewing debris. They scattered it all over his driveway and in his front yard.

CoCo yanked out red, purple and teal-colored streamers from a party he had thrown. She began wrapping the streamers around the bushes on the front lawn.

Laramie was chortling while kicking cans here and there.

CoCo said **RUN**, it's your uncle!

Dogscrimination

He was driving up Robinson Road toward his house.

They hid behind the bushes next door and watched him pull in his driveway.

He had to stop just beyond the edge because there were cans and all sorts of rubbish prohibiting him from getting to his garage. He got out of his car and said oy, those raccoons are a menace!

Laramie and CoCo were rolling in the grass laughing. They hopped up, did their happy dance and exclaimed raccoons BUSTED! They romped off traveling through the back yards of other neighbors singing "All I Wanna Do" by Sheryl Crow.

When they got to the Arnstein's house, Gengi Jo, their black teacup Pomeranian, was hiding in the gladiolus garden.

They simultaneously asked Gengi Jo what was wrong.

Jafra

I'm taking cover from Candice and she's allergic to gladiolus. She'll never look for me here 'cause her face'll swell up like a balloon at a Macy's Thanksgiving Day Parade.

They saw Candice Arnstein racing about calling Gengi Jo, Gengi Jo Arnstein, you come here this instant.

They fully understood why Gengi Jo would hide from Candice. Candice Arnstein was eight years old. She had course black hair with blunt, straight bangs and she ordinarily wore French braided pigtails with bows on the ends of each. She, more often than not, sported a gold tiara she had worn a couple of Halloweens ago. (Anyone who *really* knew her thought she should be wearing red horns.) She had freckles on her cheeks and wore yellow glasses with thick round lens. She consistently wore overalls with a tutu around her waist, and hot pink ballet slippers. Her appearance was farcical. If ever a girl needed a makeover, it was unquestionably she. She was an only child and the brattiest kid on the block. Laramie had long ago christened her "Bad Candice".

Bad Candice saw them and taunted:

> CoCo puff, CoCo puff
>
> You can't even ruff, ruff, ruff!
>
> Laramie, Laramie
>
> You're so lame,
>
> You can't even spell your name!

Then snorted while she laughed.

Mrs. Arnstein, donning the latest Dolce & Gabanna dress, styled with coordinating Jimmy Choos and Gucci purse, sashayed outside. Candice darling, it's time to go.

A roaring **NOOOOOOOOOOOOOOOOOOOO!**

Candice, love, we must go purchase a birthday present for Tia's party this afternoon.

Wrap up one of my toys for her and buy *me* a new one.

Dear, that is not proper etiquette. We shall purchase her gift and a new toy for you too. Now chop, chop. Into their silver Maserati GranTurismo and off they sped.

The Arnsteins had an in-ground swimming pool that was shaped like a lagoon. They had constructed a children's pool for Bad Candice.

Laramie saw a pitcher of lemonade on their picnic table and she poured it into Bad Candice's pool, creating the illusion *someone* had peed in it. Bad Candice had no friends who would play at her house, so her parents would assume that *someone* was she.

Dude, seriously? That's revolting!

Affirmative. Not only was she atrocious to Gengi Jo and us today, don't forget the day Bad Candice painted your tail with white shoe polish and mine with black polish. We both had to go to the groomer to get it off. Lest you forget the day she picked up Gengi Jo's poop, planted it on her parents' welcome mat and blamed it on you. Her parents called your parents and you were punished!

Oh, yeah, that had escaped me. I didn't get any bone marrow treats for one whole week. CoCo called out, yoo hoo, to starling families who were hanging out in the huge magnolia tree that shaded Bad Candice's swing set. Hey starlings, come shower the swing set.

They certainly didn't have issue with that as Bad Candice was notorious for hurling pebbles at them. They proceeded to grant CoCo's request.

Laramie said pee-u, that's disgusting. You can't see the swing set for all of the bird poop. Take that Bad Candice!

They did their happy dance.

Laramie said hey, let's go over to Pinky Russell's house.

Pinky Russell was a brown mixed breed about the size of a pug. When he was a puppy, he was abandoned by humans on a cold winter's day. As it started to snow, he became so cold and tired that he curled up in the snow and drifted off to sleep. The storm was so harsh, Dr. Russell couldn't drive and had to hike home from his office. He observed a pink, tiny object just ahead. As he grew nearer, he realized it was the pink pads of a puppy's paw peeking out of the snow. With his glove-covered hands he scooped up the shivering puppy, wrapped him in his blue, white and grey plaid cashmere scarf and carried him home. Pinky's lived there ever since.

They howled and barked and chanted:

Pinky, Pinky, we're all pals,

Come out, come out

And see us gals!

There was no response. They presumed he had gone to work with his dad. His folks were super cordial. They kept a water bowl, treat bowl and food bowl on their carport. It wasn't stealing 'cause there was a sign with a sketch of a bowl filled with dog treats and written underneath:

Welcome Pinky's Friends!
Mi casa es su casa!

After they had a snack at Pinky's, CoCo said let's go to my house and watch television.

Jafra

Coolio!

On their trek, Curly Joe, the Vandergriff's black cockapoo, lunged from a hydrangea bush and shouted BOO!

The girls didn't flinch. In a snooty tone they said oh, hi Curly Joe.

Holy crap! What are you two doing?

We're headed to CoCo's house to watch TV.

BORING! Hey ya, howsabout I tag along.

Why do you want to join us if it's *boring?*

Holy crap! Girls don't know *anything!* It will be **BORING** without *me*.

With eyebrows raised, the girls glanced at each other.

CoCo gestured her front paws with pads up, shrugged her shoulders and said, uh, gee Curly Joe, although I'm sure we'll die of boredom without you, I can't have boys over unless my humans are home.

Dogscrimination

Holy crap! Your humans are living in the Dark Ages but **WHATEVER**. It's your loss.

Once they were out of Curly Joe's sight, Laramie said fast thinking CoCo.

Thanks. If Curly Joe came over we'd be asphyxiated by obnoxious.

They entered through CoCo's pet door.

CoCo turned on the television and said hey, the "Top 10 Lap Dogs" is just starting. They sat side by side in the recliner and began viewing the program.

Look CoCo, it's your breed! I wonder if I'm in the top 10.

Indubitably. Laramie, AKA, I'm running away from home 'cause I don't get enough attention, boo hoo.

Cut it out!

As CoCo had predicted, Bichons were included. They were both disheartened to learn what they did.

I didn't know Bichons were used in the circus. That's abhorrent! Animals should never be in circuses.

Why do you say that Laramie?

Because that lifestyle is alien to animals. It's tyrannical for humans to subject animals to perform in circuses. Tigers, elephants, bears, dogs and other animals don't want to ride bicycles, stand on their heads, balance on balls or any other ludicrous stunts humans make 'em do. Circus animals are confined on a daily basis. They have to travel on trains or trailers during any and all inclement weather.

Sometimes they go without water and food for extended periods of time. Circus animals live in cages where they eat, sleep, pee and poop. There have been circus animals who have died in slavery because of deplorable living conditions.

Elephants are family oriented. They like to walk miles and miles in a day but in the circus they're chained for hours upon hours at a time. In their instinctive terrain, the male and female calves live with their mothers. The males ultimately venture out on their own and the females forever stay with their moms. The circus separates the moms from their babies at birth. They torture the babies to break their spirit and coerce them to perform feats they don't enjoy.

That's immoral!

That's an understatement. The tigers have to jump through rings of fire. They're whipped by the trainers and intimidated into obeying. The circus animals' teeth are pulled when the humans perceive them as a threat. The circus is NO place for an animal.

Jafra

I absolutely agree. The Three-Ring Circus of Bleubeau and Benno is in town this week and tonight is the premiere.

For real? Let's go crash it.

Laramie and CoCo headed to the coliseum. They went to the private parking garage and slipped in. There were cages of animals lined up as far as they could see. Laramie said follow me and she walked up to a tiger's cage. Hi, I'm Laramie and this is my friend CoCo. We oppose any circus that exploits animals.

Nice to meet you. I'm a Sumatran tiger and my name is Tut. It's refreshing to know there are creatures against circuses with animals 'cause it's really a miserable life. I'll bet I traveled 25,000 miles last year. I can't tell you how frightening it is to jump through rings of fire. I'm petrified not to because the trainers will whip me with a straight whip or lunge whip. Doesn't matter which one they use as they both hurt.

The girls both cried while they listened to Tut describe his wretched fate.

Laramie said I would put an end to this if I could Tut. One thing CoCo & I can do is stop the show tonight. Bye Tut.

The girls ran through the parking garage. They heard someone weeping. They tracked the sound to find a baby elephant lying on her tummy. There were four posts and each of her legs were tied to a post.

Laramie introduced CoCo and herself to the baby elephant.

Through her tears she whimpered, oh, my name is Sheba. I miss, sniff, sniff, I miss my mom.

Laramie observed open wounds on Sheba's body and asked what caused them.

The trainer said he had to demoralize me as he hooked me with a bull hook. The hook made jagged cuts on me. The other wound is from an electric shock prod. He did that 'cause I escaped and was searching for my mom.

Oh, you poor baby! We're gonna stop the show tonight, Sheba. Gotta run.

They ended up backstage. CoCo, with her front arms crossed while tapping her back left paw on the floor, said exactly *how* do you propose we stop this show?

Like this and she pulled the fire alarm which was attached to the automatic water sprinkler. The alarm was ear-piercing and the water was so cold it unnerved the entire audience. People were running and screaming in search of exit doors to flee the coliseum. It was categorical mayhem.

Laramie rubbed her front paws together and with a mischievous laugh, ha ha ha, no circus tonight!

Dogscrimination

As they trotted back to CoCo's house, they thought about the horror of the circus animals' lives. Although they knew it wasn't much, at least the suffering circus animals didn't have to perform that night.

When they got back to CoCo's, Laramie said I'm hungry. Do you have any snacks?

Sure, let's go to the kitchen.

CoCo pushed a chair to the cabinets, hopped up on the chair and climbed onto the counter top. One by one, she pulled vanilla pudding cups out of the cupboard and dropped them to the tile floor. Each cup burst and splat, splat, splat, as it hit the floor. The floor was covered in pudding. She jumped off the counter top, slid and rolled in the pudding, across the floor and slammed into the trash can knocking it over. There were coffee grounds that spilled out and adhered to CoCo's pudding-soaked fur. She looked like a vanilla ice cream bar that had been sprinkled with crushed chocolate wafers.

About that time, they both heard the garage door opening. Her parents were home!

CoCo said save yourself!

Laramie exited through the doggie door and ran as fast as she could to the dog park. She retired under a symmetrically-shaped maple tree. She began licking pudding off her paws while reflecting on the episodes of the day. She felt rather guilty deserting CoCo to face the music alone and hoped her folks didn't ground her. She nodded off under the tree.

Chapter Three

Interesting Encounters

Laramie awoke to the beguiling recital of a mockingbird and an exquisite sunrise. She yawned and stretched. Mornin' mockingbird. You have an impressively large repertoire. You must have been practicing for years.

Name's Sid and no, I haven't been practicing for

years. I'm only a year old. I'm a musical prodigy.

What's a musical prodigy?

I am musically inclined well beyond my years.

What's your name?

Laramie.

Did you sleep the night here?

Yes.

Don't you have a home?

I *did* have a home. I ran away.

Why would you do a silly thing like that?

'Cause of dogscrimination. It's the unfair treatment of dogs. I ran away in protest. Why did you pick this tree to sing in?

Young lady, birds don't *pick* where they sing. Birds have designated singing venues which were established long ago. I hate to think of the mess this world would be in if birds just willy nilly sang wherever they so desired! If birds had that leisure, why there would never be birds singing at garbage dumps, prison yards, cemeteries and so forth. No, no, no. Birds are given strict guidelines before they leave the nest as to where they may or may not sing. We have to provide music for the entire world you see. There's no dogscrimination with us when it comes to whom we entertain. Did I use the "d" word properly?

I'm honestly not certain. I suppose you could use it like that. Let me get this straight. Birds that live and sing at the bank aren't singing there because they're rich. The birds that sing at the fitness center aren't necessarily fit and the birds that sing at the movie theaters aren't actors and th…

Yes, yes, you get the gist.

Hmm, interesting. Seems I learn something new every day. By the way, I always see birds flying together and I've never seen any crash. How do you all keep from flying into each other?

Jafra

Bird traffic controllers, my friend. Bird traffic would be total chaos without them!

I've flown before.

Yeah, right and I've driven a car.

I have flown in a jet.

Do indulge me.

My humans adopted me through a nationwide Bichon Frise' rescue group that is based in Colorado. It's called Cotton Puff Rescue. Their goal is to get Bichons out of pet stores because most pet store dogs come from puppy mills.

What are puppy mills?

They are commercial breeding facilities for all breeds of dogs. The sole objective of the puppy mills is to make money. They don't take good care of the dogs. There are dogs that live at the puppy mills and they stay in cages unless they are breeding. After they give birth, the puppies are sold to pet stores or auctioned off. Cotton Puff

Rescue purchased Bichons from an auction at a puppy mill in Missouri. My biological mom, Annabelis, was in a group they bought. She was pregnant with me and my siblings. Annabelis was sent to a foster home in Frisco, Texas. We were all born there. When I was eleven weeks old, I flew MJ1717 from Texas to live with my humans. They named me Laramie because they were in Laramie, Wyoming when they found out my flight schedule.

They adopted you yet you abandoned th…

Suddenly, a female mockingbird flew up. She was in a panic, speaking incoherently and frantically flapping her wings.

Millie, I cannot understand what you're saying! Calm down and speak slowly.

There's, ther, there's a long, black snake slithering up the tree toward our nest and I can't stop him by myself! He's going to get our babies Sid! He's going to get our babies!

They both began squawking which drew the attention of all different bird species. There were blue jays, cardinals, chickadees, song sparrows, you name it. All types of birds flew up to see if they could help.

All of a sudden, the original "James Bond Theme" by Monty Norman began playing. A handsome crow flew up to them. The feathers of his breast were white and shaped like a bow tie. His head feathers were slicked back with hair gel which gave him a suave and debonair appearance. He said Bird, James Bird and stealthily flew to the tree where Sid and Millie's babies were dozing. Bird made it just in time to ward off the predatory snake and rescue the babies.

Sid & Millie synchronously and sighingly said thank you James Bird for saving our family!

Don't mention it, it's what I do.

Millie flew back to her babies and Sid flew back to Laramie.

Now, my newfound canine friend, pardon me, as I must resume my morning concert.

Oh, surely. It was a treat meeting you. She trotted off singing:

Laramie, oh Laramie
A little white dog named Laramie
She's so sweet, gotta meet
The little white dog named Laramie

She bellowed out, today on the Laramie Babelay Program, Laramie runs away from home in protest of dogscrimination. It's rampant across our nation.

She was really hungry and she smelled something wonderful. She was following that enticing scent and literally paying no attention to

Jafra

her surroundings. She was walking directly through a police standoff!

Beecher Palm Mize had single-handedly robbed The Last Trust Bank. He vamoosed with two children, as hostages, and they were held up in a motel room. Beecher Palm Mize had called the SWAT leader and demanded that food be sent to his room. It was that honest-to-goodness motel room harboring yummy-smelling food which was luring little Laramie.

The SWAT leader radioed to the crew and said hold your fire! There's a small white dog walking toward Beecher Palm Mize's door.

Laramie be bopped into Beecher Palm Mize's room.

The media and police officials cringed when they saw her go in. They imagined he would do unspeakable things to the little white dog.

Unbeknownst to anyone, Beecher Palm Mize was gravely afraid of dogs, any dog, large or small.

Laramie jumped on the chair next to the table of food. She stood on her hind legs, put her front paws on the table and began eating.

Beecher Palm Mize walked out of the bathroom and screamed like a little girl when he saw her.

She jumped down and started walking toward him. As she was approaching him, she was licking her lips and wagging her tail. She fully intended to properly introduce herself.

He was screaming and yelling, get back, get back, aaahh! He jumped on the bed and onto the nightstand. He picked up the phone, called the hostage negotiator and was hysterically exclaiming I'm terrified of dogs! Help me! Save me from this ferocious beast! Aaaaahhh, aaaahhh, pleeeease!

The negotiator agreed to help Beecher Palm Mize.

He told him to exit the room with his hands up.

Beecher Palm Mize put up his hands and jumped on the bed closest to the exit door, all the while screaming stay away, stay away! He bolted out of the room and was immediately handcuffed.

The young hostages ran out of the room and into the safety of their parents' arms.

Laramie sauntered out of the motel room wondering what she had done to scare that man.

The media wasn't interested in anyone but Laramie. They surrounded her, pointing microphones and cameras in her face. They were excitedly asking her all sorts of questions. Where did you come from? What's your name? Where are your humans? Why did you go to that room? Did you know there was a dangerous criminal in that room? Were you trying to save the hostages? How did you make him surrender?

She disregarded them while dancing away and

singing "Bom Bom" by Sam and the Womp.

Jafra

Dogscrimination

Chapter Four

What a Cook Out

That afternoon, she saw a couple of dogs in the near distance. One was a blue chow chow and the other was a tan Shar Pei. Hola, I'm Laramie. Who are you guys? The chow chow said my name is Chang-Nan Joe and this is my best friend Cheng Ping Ren. What are you guys up to?

Jafra

Chang-Nan Joe said we were groomed earlier and now we're headed to Cheng Ping Ren's house to hang out. His humans are gone 'til tomorrow.

Your hairstyle is too cool, Chang-Nan Joe! (He had a lion cut and it was so awesome.)

Chang-Nan Joe, real cool-like, nodded his head up with eyes closed then down with his eyes opened.

You smell good Cheng Ping Ren.

Thanks but I don't like the way I smell. I hate it when I get bathed in that girly-smelling shampoo the groomer uses.

They both asked her what she was up to.

I ran away from home in protest of dogscrimination.

Chang-Nan Joe said I've never heard of that.

It's when dogs get treated differently from humans and I'm sick of it. Dogscrimination is rampant across our nation.

Dogscrimination

Cheng Ping Ren said that sounds like an admirable cause but where do you plan to go?

I don't precisely know. I'm as the Aussies say, going on a walkabout, mate.

How about you come over to my house and hang out for bit. My house is just at the end of this cul-de-sac.

She pushes her front paws in the air and says woop woop, coolio, let's go.

They arrived at Cheng Ping Ren's house and it was a mansion. Ornate iron gates encompassed the mansion. There were two massive, marble lion statues, imported from Athens, Greece, on either side of the gated entrance. There was an enormous, octagon-shaped fountain which was framed by a lavish flower bed in the middle of the circular driveway. It was a mansion of Tudor architecture with a five car garage.

Doggie door is this way. Follow me. The garden

grounds circumscribed the mansion which led them to his entrance.

Whoa! I've never seen a doggie door like this before.

Cheng Ping Ren pushed a button to the side of the door and it automatically opened. He said welcome to my humble abode as he gestured her in with his front left paw.

Dude, all of this belongs to you? The intro of "This Must Be the Place" by The Talking Heads should be playing.

Yeppur on both points, Laramie.

You are the luckiest dog I know!

The doggie entrance opened directly into Cheng Ping Ren's own place. It was like an apartment. There were ceiling-to-floor windows overlooking the pool and gardens. There was an oblong island in the middle of the room. It had a purple granite countertop speckled in yellow, red and teal with a sink in the center. There were purple cabinets on three sides of the island and on the fourth side there was a shelf with three bowls inset. One was filled with gourmet treats, the second filled with gourmet food and the third filled with cool, filtered water. Each bowl could be refilled by the push of a button. Cheng Ping Ren pushed a button when his bowls needed cleaning. Essentially, everything he wanted was at the tips of his pads.

He had a 48" flat screen television on the wall above the fireplace. A black leather sofa was in front of the fireplace and there were two matching recliners on either side of it. There were bone-shaped pillows on the sofa and recliners. They were yellow with purple, red, black and teal paw prints.

On the opposite wall, there were toys galore. Toys Laramie had never seen before. He had Ball-

Ball, Snack Casino, A-Maze for Treat, Find & Treat, Dog Checkers and Doggie Magic. They were all from the Doggie Einstein collection. He had stuffed animals too but they were far larger than any stuffed animals she had ever seen.

Cheng Ping Ren said I understand the dogscrimination cause and all but as Eleanor Roosevelt said, "Remember, no one can make you feel inferior without your consent." He gave Laramie some hot pink, square Chanel sunglasses which fit her to a tee and they went outside.

Cheng Ping Ren got on the diving board, boing, boing, boing, and jumped into the pool. Ah, this is so refreshing! Maybe I can ditch this girly smell.

Laramie got on a float and drifted around in the pool.

Chang-Nan Joe chilled on a chaise lounge

sporting black Ray Bans. He used the remote control and turned on "Great Day" by Paul McCartney.

A few minutes later, there was a hubbub of dogs howling and barking. It was a variety of breeds from the neighborhood. There was Traveler the Border collie, Ruchi the Basenji, Jack the schnauzer, Cruz the Boston terrier, Abby Rose the silky terrier, Colton the fox terrier mix, Laurel the Irish wolfhound, Skylar the kuvasz, Esmeralda the Lhasa apso mix, Eli the Old English sheepdog, Theo the papillon, Bebes the Irish setter mix, Ike the Portuguese water dog, Sadie the standard French poodle, Moondog the shiba inu, Kojak the cockapoo and leading the pack was Pinot Grigio. Pinot Grigio, an overweight white bulldog, was barreling toward the pool. He was shouting last one in is a rotten egg! His splash was so forceful it knocked Laramie off her float and into the weeping willow.

The other dogs were running toward the pool and splash, splish, splash, splish, as they jumped in.

Laramie retrieved her glasses and got back on her float.

Pinot Grigio swam over to apologize and introduce himself.   I've never seen you in this neighborhood before.

This is the first time I've been here. I ran away from home.

Why?

'Cause of dogscrimination. It's rampant across our nation.

I have a tremendous vocabulary but I do not recognize that word. What's the denotation?

Dogs are treated unfairly by humans and I'm tired of it.

Is it in the diction...

The brouhaha of the other dogs in the pool disrupted him. They were belting *Pinot* and Pinot Grigio squealed *Grigio* as he swam to them like an Olympiad swimmer.

Pinot!

Grigio!

Nightfall was advancing when Cheng Ping Ren greeted Itchie Flanigan. Itchie Flanigan was a Chinese crested who lived next door. Itchie Flanigan was the ugliest dog any of them had ever met. His fur looked like he had combed it with a firecracker and his eyes bulged out of his head about the size of muscadine grapes. He had a skin problem that itched profusely and prompted him to scratch most all the time, thus he earned the name Itchie Flanigan. Itchie, for obvious reasons and Flanigan was his adopted surname. Of course, they all adored Itchie Flanigan. He was only hideous on the outside.

Itchie Flanigan would share his toys and treats without anybody even asking him. He was really funny. He was mad about singing and dancing. He changed the music to "Thriller" by Michael Jackson and led them in the dance.

As the guests were dancing, Cheng Ping Ren put on a chef's hat and an apron. The apron had a photo of a grill and written underneath:

"Master's Grill"

Below that was a photo of a Cheng Ping Ren and written underneath:

"Grill Master"

He grilled hamburgers and hot dogs. Naturally, the bulk of the company requested their burgers be rare.

The guests all savored their meal and comradery. While they were helping clean up, Itchie Flanigan said hey, let's go over to miser Crapsalotti's mansion.

Laramie asked who.

Cheng Ping Ren said it's Mr. Capsalotti. We call him miser Crapsalotti because he's a moneygrubbing, depraved, old man. He always wears a black suit, he walks with his shoulders slumped over and he sweeps his greasy, long hair over his bald scalp. He's never worked a day in his life. He inherited all of his money. He treats his household servants like slaves and they say if he pays anyone for anything, he thinks he owns them. They call his house Crapsalotti Correctional Compound, Triple C for short, because working there is like being in prison. He doesn't take responsibility of anything he does wrong. He invariably blames other people for his mistakes and bad decisions. He always claims to be the victim in any confrontation or argument when he's repeatedly the instigator. He is a hoarder of cars, furniture, jewels, clothes and all sorts of other material items, which doesn't bother us. What angers us is he collects dogs. Dogs are not things. Dogs are living creatures with feelings, thoughts and ideas. He doesn't expend any time with the dogs he accumulates. He merely stashes them all in crates. He brags about the dogs he possesses, their champion bloodlines and how much he paid for them. Sometimes, he's gone for weeks at a time and doesn't make arrangements for anyone to care for them. Some have gotten ill and others even died while he was gone. Neighbors have called the police but even they're afraid of him he's so evil. Laramie said aha, a calamitous case of dogscrimination but we shouldn't go over there. Itchie Flanigan stated don't be a square, while drawing an air-square with his front paws.

Dogscrimination

The crowd murmured in agreement that it was, de facto, dogscrimination. They marched to miser Crapsalotti's house. They were opening the crates and releasing dogs when miser Crapsalotti emerged from the shadows. Itchie Flanigan ran in front of him stumbling him and he partially landed into the Great Dane's crate. Traveler, the Border collie, pushed him in. Sadie, the standard French poodle, closed the door and locked it with a padlock she saw next to the crate.

Miser Crapsalotti was commanding them, get me out of this crate!

They were all laughing at him which only incensed him further.

Traveler said you don't scare us. We have no interest in your money, jewels, cars or anything else, miser Crapsalotti. You chill in there and think about the inhumane demeanor you've favored the precious dogs in your life.

The crowd cheered **hear, hear**, dispersed and went their separate ways.

Cheng Ping Ren invited Laramie to stay at his place so they headed back to his mansion. They went to his room and started watching "Blackfish", a documentary about Tilikum, the orca. They were both appalled to learn about the barbaric treatment of killer whales in captivity. The innocent whales are prisoners for the veritable amusement of humans.

Laramie started crying when she saw how the calves were abducted from their families. She said I cannot believe the horrific lives these creatures have. It's as bad as the way animals are abused in circuses.

It depressed them to hear that every aspect of the captive whales' natural lives are dismantled by incarceration. Captive whales are restricted to swimming circles in concrete tanks, but in the wild, they swim up to 100 miles per day. The whales don't live as long in captivity as they would in their natural habitat. Their dorsal fins collapse in captivity but not in their familiar haven. They have intricate social lives in their innate environment. They are highly intelligent and emotional. They have strong family ties but in captivity those bonds are severed.

Cheng Ping Ren said any business that uses animals for entertainment is corrupt and should be outlawed!

Indeed!

Not long after the documentary ended, they caught forty winks.

The following morning, they ate a hearty breakfast.

Laramie asked Cheng Ping Ren if he would like to go with her.

No thanks. I treasure my life here. Subsequently,

I am quite selective as to how I utilize my time. As Carl Sandburg wrote, "Time is the coin of your life. It is the only coin you have, and only you can determine how it will be spent. Be careful lest you let people spend it for you."

Whoa, deep. Thank you for your generous hospitality.

Chapter Five

Jocelyn

Laramie was promenading about and wound up at a shopping center. She stood on her back legs and looked in the window of each store. Gazing into the window of Z Mart, she observed a machine filled with stuffed animals. Although she would never admit it, she was beginning to feel homesick for her parents, Floyd and her toys. She ambled through the automatic sliding door and into the portal of the toy machine. She opted for a stuffed raccoon. She was exiting the machine when an employee saw her and began chasing her, yelling thief, thief! Somebody stop that dog with the raccoon! Laramie was running as fast as her short legs could carry her. A boy tried to catch her but she escaped his clutches. She ran between an employee's legs causing him to trip and drop the box of marbles he was carrying. Laramie exited through a side door, abandoning the humanoids slipping and sliding on the marbles.

She said yikes, that was close! She walked for hours carrying her raccoon. Suddenly the sky became dark and she knew all too well what was impending. Mother Nature was busy and a storm she-was-a-brewin'. Laramie was terrified of storms. She was running as it began raining, thundering and lightening. She spotted an opened garage door and zoomed in. She was trembling so forcefully that her teeth were chattering.

A little girl with long blonde hair and green eyes walked out of the house and into the garage. She saw Laramie and gasped in delight. Who are you? You are so pretty! (She talked superfast, taking little to no pauses in between.) My name is Jocelyn, what's your name? Oh, it doesn't matter, you'll be Margaret. I've forevermore wanted a dog but my mom said no and even if I could have a dog I absolutely could not call it Margaret because our next door neighbor, who I really like, is named Margaret and my mom said Margaret wouldn't appreciate having a dog named after her which I disagree. As Jocelyn continued gabbing, she got a towel and dried off

Laramie's fur. Margaret, what in the world were you doing outside by yourself?

I ran away from home.

Why?

Because of dogscrimination. It's rampant across our nation and I'm protesting it.

Dog what?

Dogscrimination. It's the unfair treatment of dogs.

Oh good grief. You must stay here with me, Margaret. You won't be dogscriminated here. My mom is a widow. She works out of town every week, only home on the weekends and my nanny, Blair, is preoccupied watching TV instead of me. I'll sneak you into my room. It will be sanfrantabulous. We'll have lots of fun and I'll dress you up in doll clothes and I'll bring food and water to you and we'll be BFF's and we...

Laramie interrupted her, whoa, whoa, whoa, whoa, whoa, whoa, whoa. Thanks for drying me off and all but my name is Laramie. I don't know what widow means or what a nanny is. What the what is a BFF? Definitely no doll clothes and I...

No, no, no, you *will be* Margaret. My mom was married to my dad and he died which converted my mom from wife to widow. My mom says a nanny is merely an expensive version of a babysitter. She says Blair really isn't even worth babysitter fees because she knows Blair doesn't pay any attention to me. She's either on the phone, on the internet, listening to music, watching TV, anything but taking care of me. BFF is best friends forever and oh, you'll look adorable in the doll clothes I have. We'll have tea parties, play board games and pretend games. Sssshhhh, be immensely quiet until we get to my bedroom. Jocelyn picked up Laramie directly under her front legs and her back legs were dragging the ground as Jocelyn was tiptoeing through the house. After they passed the room Blair was in, Laramie grunted and wiggled from Jocelyn's grip. She shook her entire body and said I can walk on my own already!

Oh, okay Margaret, that's fine, tiptoe, sssshhhhh and follow me. They quietly tiptoed through her house until they arrived at Jocelyn's room and she opened her bedroom door.

Laramie was amazed how lavish her room was. The walls were a whisper of pink. She had a king size bed with a canopy. The comforter was pink with red ballerina silhouettes and the canopy was draped with teal sheers. The view of the mountains from her bay view window was stunning. She had the complete pink crackle furniture collection from Z Mart's toy department. She had the dining table with chairs, two rocking chairs, toy chest, standing mirror, pantry and a time out chair. The dining table was set with white Kate Spade china that had pink tea roses along the edges and a matching tea set. There was a cream colored sofa with a pink, red and teal throw neatly draped along the top. In front of the sofa was a glass teardrop coffee table with a pink ballerina figurine on it. She had her own flat screen TV, computer, iPad, iPhone, dolls, stuffed animals and any other imaginable thing a seven year old does not require to exist happily yet Jocelyn didn't seem happy. In fact, she seemed quite lonely.

Jocelyn lifted the top of her pink crackle toy chest and was sorting through doll clothes. She slipped a yellow nightgown with orange Gerber daisies and purple butterflies over Laramie's head which concealed her bandana. She put a matching night cap on her head and said let's watch TV. They got in the gorgeous canopy bed and watched cartoons until they dozed off.

The next morning, Laramie was awakened by Jocelyn scrambling through her closet. She was selecting her attire for the day. She chose a pair of powder puff blue leggings; a chocolate brown skirt; a sleeveless, powder puff blue turtleneck; and brown combat-style boots. She braided her hair in a fishtail braid and tied a powder puff blue bow with brown polka dots at the end of the braid. Then she began rummaging through the pink crackle toy chest. She chose a purple chiffon dress with a petticoat and a lavender floral hat with purple bow and veil. She put the petticoat on Laramie and then the dress. Once she tied the bow on the back of the dress, she put the hat on her and said oh, Margaret this is simply divine! Let's have a tea party, shall we?

Although the petticoat was itchy and the veil tickled her nose, Laramie was hungry and thirsty, so she acquiesced.

Sit here Margaret and don't put your elbows on the table.

She mimicked Jocelyn's every move. She unfolded the pink linen napkin and laid it on her lap.

Margaret took the teapot and poured NOTHING into Laramie's cup. Then she placed NOTHING on Laramie's plate.

Laramie was blankly staring at Jocelyn.

She said well, don't stand on ceremony. You may begin.

Begin what, missy? There's NOTHING in my cup or on my plate.

There's tea in your cup and delicious lemon cookies on your plate. We're *pretending* Margaret.

I'm not pretending to be thirsty and hungry so this fictitious food isn't helpful!

Oh my. I've never had anything *living* to play with. It didn't occur to me that you may be ravenous.

Jocelyn pulled a lavender bib out of the toy chest and tied it around Laramie's neck. Then she went to her pink crackle pantry, took out a jar of Jett's baby food, opened it and began spoon feeding her. She dipped the spoon into the food and then made a train noise, **wooo wooo, chug a chug a chug a chug, a wooo wooo,** while moving the spoon toward Laramie's mouth. Next the baby food-filled spoon was zooming around in the air while Jocelyn made a swishing noise, said **coming in for a landing** and into her mouth with the spoon.

Laramie was so famished that she didn't mind.

After the last morsel was consumed, Jocelyn sat in the rocking chair and said Margaret, come over here. She cradled Laramie in her arms and yes, you guessed it, put the nipple of a water-filled baby bottle in her mouth. Jocelyn was vigorously rocking back and forth while rapidly singing:

Row, row, row your boat
Gently down the stream,
Merrily, merrily, merrily, merrily
Life is but a dream

Laramie, obviously not accustomed to a bottle or the rigorous rocking back and forth, became choked and started coughing. Jocelyn tossed her around placing her head on her shoulder, began patting her back and saying there, there.
Laramie lost control and **buuuuurrrrrppp**. Embarrassingly, she said I, ya, pardon me.

Margaret, how uncouth! Pointing to the pink crackle time out chair facing the corner while saying time out for you.

But, I, ya …

No buts young lady. Time out for you!

What seemed like an eternity later, Jocelyn was tapping her hand on the seat of the pink crackle chair in front of her pink crackle vanity and motioning for Laramie to sit there.

Laramie relinquished the time out chair and moved to the vanity chair.

Jocelyn put on some music. She removed the hat and dress. She was singing "This Ain't Your Mama's Broken Heart" by Miranda Lambert while brushing Laramie's fur. As she was singing, she worked mousse through Laramie's fur, long ears and fluffy tail. Then she applied purple hair chalk on her fur, she teased the fur and spritzed it with hairspray. Perfect! She redressed Laramie. She took a nail file and filed Laramie's nails on all four paws, much to Laramie's dismay. Then she began painting Laramie's nails with purple glitter nail polish.

As Jocelyn was blowing on her nails to dry them, she said it's probably time for you to use the bathroom.

Oh, well, as a matter of fact, yes I do need to go and my mom told me it happens to the best of us. She began singing to the tune of "Jeepers Creepers" by Louis Armstrong:

Poo poo, poo poo
I really need to poo poo
Poo poo, poo poo
I really need to G-O

Jocelyn was getting something out of the toy chest and cutting it with scissors. She started walking toward Laramie while saying Margaret, lie down.

Jafra

Laramie's eyes were as big as half dollars when she saw Jocelyn was holding a diaper with a hole cut out for her tail. Laramie, excitedly, no no no no no no no! This is where I unequivocally draw the line. I don't care how lonely you are. I want to use the bathroom, outside, like every other civilized dog in the world.

Heavens no Margaret. This is like "Hotel California" by The Eagles. Leaving is not an option.

Laramie was walking backwards and working her way to the bedroom door. She hurriedly turned to the door, opened it and began running through the house. As she was running, she was taking off the dress, then the petticoat and tossing it up in the air. She was shouting this **is** dogscrimination and it's rampant across our nation! The petticoat was flying through the air. It landed on a vintage Fukagaw Arita Japanese porcelain vase, toppling it over and crashing onto the floor into a zillion pieces.

Blair was entering the front door from checking the mailbox only to find Laramie running and Jocelyn right behind her.

Jocelyn was out of breath, saying wait, wa, come back Margaret, let me put, put this diaper on you. Blair swatted Laramie on her bottom with the mail as she leapt through the door and fled as fast as she could. She didn't decelerate until Jocelyn's house was well out of sight. Unfortunately, she left her raccoon behind. Thankfully, she had managed to retain her red bandana that had white bones outlined in purple on it.

Dogscrimination

Chapter Six

Running With the Big Dogs

She walked for hours and she began singing "Laramie Dog" to the tune of "Jingle Bell Rock" by Bobby Helms:

Laramie, Laramie, Laramie dog

Laramie dog is a Bichon dog

Snugly & furry & white as can be

Jafra

The nicest dog that you'll ever meet

Laramie, Laramie, Laramie dog

Laramie dog is a Bichon dog

Cuddly & fuzzy & nice as can be

The smartest dog that you'll ever meet

The Laramie dog is a flea-free dog

Who'll bark the night away

Bark bark bark bark bark

The Laramie dog is a flea-free dog

She'll go barkin' all night and day

Laramie, Laramie, Laramie dog

Laramie dog is just great

A bark and a growl and a sniffity sniff

That's the Laramie, that's the Laramie, that's the

Laramie dog

A gruff voice bellowed what is that racket? Laramie stopped in her tracks and spun around to see a Great Pyrenees in the field of a farm. It's me, Laramie, I'm a Bichon Frise'. I'm running away from home and was singing as I was moving along.

Why is a pretty little thing like you running away?

Because I'm tired of dogscrimination.

What on earth is that?

It's what my humans do to me. They dogscriminate against me.

I don't understand.

They go places without me. They say I'm not welcome. In fact, no dogs allowed. The other day, I found out they're going to see a movie without me. I realized that is dogscrimination and dogscrimination is rampant across our nation. I decided to run away from home. What's your name?

I'm Private Wilson Pyrenees but my friends call me Willie. It is short for Wilson and since I love

Willie Nelson. I want to be a musician but my humans make me work in this field protecting their goats. Goats are okay but I'm, achoo, allergic to them. I see other dogs riding along in the car with their humans. My humans never take me anywhere. I don't even go to the veterinarian's office because our veterinarian makes house calls. I've been dogscriminated against my whole life. I'm going to run away from home and join you.

Excellent!

Laramie and Willie had traveled for a few hours when Willie began singing "On the Road Again", by his hero, Willie Nelson. He altered some of the words:

On the road again -

Just can't wait to get on the road again.

The life I love is digging bones with my friends

And I can't wait to get on the road again.

On the road again

Goin' places that I've never been.

Peein' on things that I may never p'on again

And I can't wait to get on the road again.

On the road again -

Like a pack of wolves we head on down the highway

We're the best of friends.

Insisting that the world keep turning our way

And our way

is on the road again.

Just can't wait to get on the road again.

The life I love is chasin' cars with my friends

And I can't wait to get on the road again.

On the road again

Like a pack of wolves we head on down the highway

We're the best of friends

Insisting that the world keep turning our way

And our way

Jafra

And I can't wait to get on the road again.

Of course after a few lines, Laramie was singing along. Willie, that's a great song, woof, wooooof!

Slow down there, little Laramie. What's that ahead of us?

Several police cars.

As they drew in closer to the scene, they still couldn't determine what was going on.

Laramie noticed they were standing next to a police car that had "K-9" on it. What's K-9?

Not sure.

A deep voice from inside the vehicle snapped it's an acronym. *K-9 for canine* and indicates there's a police dog in the car.

They peered up to the back window of the cruiser and saw a handsome Belgian Malinois.

I'm Laramie and this is Willie. Who are you?

I'm Belgian Bomber, nickname's BB.

Dogscrimination

Willie said man, you have a cool job.

BB exclaimed, COOL JOB? I HATE my job! I do not like guns. Guns are just wrong, man. Besides that, riding in a car makes me ill. Front seat, back seat, heck I could be driving and I would get car sick. I think it's an inner ear issue.

Laramie asked BB what he wanted to do.

I want to be a stay-at-home dog. I want to live in a big city so my human and I won't need a car. We can walk everywhere we want to go. We can dine at outside cafes, have picnics in parks and revel in all the excitements a thriving metropolis bestows its populace.

Willie said we're running away from home.

Why?

We're tired of being dogscriminated.

Like, what's that, man?

Humans treat dogs unfairly and we're not allowed many places. We're tired of dogscrimination. Dogscrimination is rampant across our nation.

Laramie said go with us BB.

Willie nosed open the door and BB jumped out.

They all ran away yelling dogscrimination is rampant across our nation.

BB led them to a drab, grey, concrete block building enclosed by a chain link fence. The paint on the building was chipping, the landscaping was overgrown with weeds and the parking lot needed restriping.

Laramie asked where they were.

This is the animal shelter, man.

Laramie curiously said animal shelter.

Yes, animal shelter, man. It's where humans put unwanted animals. If an animal is roaming around, the critter cop will arrest it and put it in here. It's jail for animals but they usually only stay for three days.

Laramie was beyond perplexed. Where do they go after three days?

Like, if they aren't adopted or claimed by their owner, the humans euthanize them, man.

Youfa what?

They murder them, man.

WHAT? WHY?

Man, there's not enough homes for many of them so they annihilate them.

Why are animals overpopulated?

In a word, HUMANS! Countless mortals are irresponsible pet owners or pet breeders. Instead of having their pets spayed or neutered they continue to let animals breed. There are limited homes for all of them, man.

Laramie said we have to liberate them. I'm sure you have a way in, BB.

Of course I can get in but see the sign on the door, man:

SHELTER CLOSED TODAY

PET ADOPTION EVENT

AT

PETS-R-A-BIG DEAL

BB stood on a crate and looked in the window. Oh man, I see one dog in there. I'll bet he hasn't been here ample time to attend the adoption function. Once a month, Pets-R-A-Big Deal invites the animal shelter to bring the three-day animals to the store in hopes of adopting them out.

Save him!

Okay, okay, Laramie.

BB had been to the animal shelter with his police officer after hours once before and he remembered the code. He pawed 7 5 1 0, the door opened and they sneaked in.

Dogscrimination

As they wandered through the building, the faint singing they heard became louder. The dog was singing "Yesterday" by The Beatles.

BB said shh, stop that singing, man!

The dog stopped singing. He yelped out who are you? What do you want from me?

Laramie skipped to the cage and was aghast to find a dog that looked much like her. What she saw before her eyes was uncanny! It was as if she were looking in a mirror. In fact if the incarcerated dog had a red bandana with white bones outlined in purple on it, she would think she was looking at herself. I'm Laramie. Are you a Bichon Frise'?

Yeppur. My name is Reggie but I want to be called Ringo.

Why?

My humans named me Reggie but I'm into music. I want to be called Ringo, like the Beatle.

How on earth did you end up here if you have humans?

I was eight weeks old when they adopted me from my biological mom. They were sooooo nice to me when they first took me to their house, my new home. I was there briefly when the man of the house began getting angry with me. I tried not to have accidents in the house but no one listened when I told them I needed to go out. Not long after I moved there, the children stopped playing with me. I guess I was like a toy to them and my newness wore off. In the evening they would gate off the stairs. They would go upstairs to watch TV, play board games or do homework. I was left downstairs all alone. Essentially they ignored me.

After a few years, I decided I had had enough. I thought there must be a human somewhere in the world who would want me and dote over me and cherish me. I did what any lonely being might do. I ran away from house.

You ran away from *home*.

No, house. A home is supposed to be warm and loving. Anyway, I was arrested on 17th Street last night by a critter cop and he brought me here.

They heard a vehicle drive up.

Willie said it's the critter cop. We gotta scram!

Laramie opened Ringo's crate.

They all took off running into the pleasant spring evening.

All the while, Laramie was yelling dogscrimination is rampant across our nation.

Ringo said thanks for bustin' me out of the slammer. What's dogscrimination?

All roared it's the unfair treatment of dogs.

They pressed on to the dog park to slumber.

They curled up under the stars when BB said I can't sleep.

Ringo said me either.

Willie said let's play "Animated Object You Wouldn't Wanna Be".

Laramie said I'll go first. A fire hydrant.

Everyone asked why she wouldn't wanna be a fire hydrant.

'Cause you would always be getting peed on.

Giggling, Willie said a mailbox.

They asked why he wouldn't wanna be a mailbox.

You're outside in all types of weather, you never know when a car will run into you or a kid will bash you with a baseball bat.

Ringo said a penny.

They asked why he wouldn't wanna be a penny.

Even though you add up to dollars, nobody wants ya.

BB said a vacuum cleaner.

They asked why he wouldn't wanna be a vacuum

cleaner.

You never know what you're gonna be forced to
eat.

Laramie said I wouldn't want to be a shopping
cart.

They asked why she wouldn't wanna be a
shopping cart.

'Cause you're hit by cars. You have to stay out in
all kinds of weather until someone pushes you
inside. Babies with dirty diapers sit in you.

Willie said speaking of diapers …

All laughing until, one by one, they drifted off to
sleep.

Dogscrimination

Chapter Seven

Going To a Party

The next morning, they ventured off singing, dancing and giggling. They were having the time of their lives when they came upon a magnificent brindle pit bull. They were all somewhat leery to approach her because pit bulls get such a bad rap from some humans but Laramie marched right up to her.

Jafra

Hi, I'm Laramie. What's your name?

They noticed the dog was quivering.

She replied Killer. My name is Killer.

BB said you must be a vicious dog.

She softly replied, no, no I'm not. I dislike my name. I wish my name was Ruby, like an elegant gem. She sighed my existence is consumed with vacant hope.

Laramie asked Ruby why she said that.

I'm perpetually chained to this tree. No one ever talks to me or pets me. Sometimes they forget to feed me. My water bowl is either empty or in the sun or too far away for me to reach.

BB asked her what happened to her head.

I was barking last night 'cause there was an intruder outside my human's house. I was trying to protect my human, his family and property. My human came out and kicked me in the head a few times while shouting shut up. He kept kicking me and saying shut up you stupid, ugly, good-for-nothing dog! My head still hurts from the beating and my eyes are swollen from crying all night.

Laramie said that's dogscrimination. You must come with us to protest it.

What?

It's dogs being unfairly treated by humans. We're all running away.

Oh, I don't think I could make a decision like that.

Laramie said if you don't make a decision that in itself is a decision.

Ringo quickly unlatched Ruby from her chain.

They skedaddled off yelling dogscrimination is rampant across our nation.

They decided to go to Pets-R-A-Big Deal and BB led the way. They concurred no one would notice them if they appeared to be with a human. So they all nonchalantly walked in the front door along with humans entering the store. They strolled to the center of the store and saw all of the shelter animals. They each opened crates and released them. They all started running toward the front door howling and barking, which only brought unneeded attention to themselves.

Laramie was yelling dogscrimination is rampant across our nation.

The employees were running after the animals, to no avail. The shelter animals went one direction and the protestors in another.

The protestors finally stopped under a mighty oak tree.

Ruby said good gracious that was close.

Willie said I'm hungry.

It was unanimous they must have some food and water.

Laramie asked where they could eat.

BB said follow me, I know where we can eat.

Once they arrived, Laramie said it's Barney's Burger Bun. No shirt, no shoes, no service. More pertinently, NO DOGS ALLOWED. Even if we *could* go in, we don't have any money.

Man, just follow me to the back. The employees throw out food that is thoroughly pristine. The feral cats who live around these dumpsters eat here. Actually, the food is so good the freegans eat here.

Willie asked what freegans are.

It's humans who dumpster dive for food.

Ruby said I don't feel comfortable stealing food from those poor feral cats or the freegans.

BB explained that the feral cats, as well as freegans, have a philosophy of live and let live. They don't mind sharing.

As they approached the dumpsters, they only saw one big white cat with black paws and it looked like he was wearing boots. He was napping under the tree adjacent to a dumpster. He opened one eye and said whatup dogs.

Hi, I'm Laramie. These are my friends Willie, BB, Ringo and Ruby. We're famished and need something to eat.

I'm Mr. Boots. You're welcome to all you can eat. You're a motley crew. What are you canines up to?

She said we're running away from home 'cause of dogscrimination.

Indeed. I'm not sure what that is but it sounds like quite an adventure.

Willie said it's the unfair treatment of dogs.

Oh.

After they finished eating they thanked Mr. Boots.

He invited them to a party.

Laramie asked what kind of party.

Oh, a bunch of us ferals and forest creatures

gather around and take turns singing. Sometimes, we pick up "The Critter Town Criar" and take turns reading. We party way into the night and generally all just camp out 'til morning. Are you sure we won't be dogscriminated at the party?

Never. Although the humans think otherwise, we all generally get along fairly well.

Laramie asked whatcha think gang.

Simultaneous responses, yes, sure, I'm game and I'm in.

Mr. Boots led the way.

The protestors followed him and called out dogscrimination is rampant across our nation.

Along the way, they saw a miniature pinscher/Manchester terrier mix trotting along. They stopped and Laramie said hiya fella. What's your name?

Name is Zephyr.

They all asked where he was headed.

He shrugged his shoulders and said I dunno. Anywhere but home.

Laramie asked if he was being dogscriminated against at home.

Dunno. What's that?

It's humans treating us dogs like we're not as good. They leave us home alone and go do fun things. They eat different food from us. I could go on and on Zephyr. In fact, that's why we're all running away.

I loved my home 'til my Pop fell head over heels for someone. His girlfriend brought her dog to live with us and that dog is downright nasty to me. Portia, that's her name, is a golden retriever/Irish setter mix. She bullies me, steals my toys, eats my food and humiliates me in front of my friends. Sure I'll go with you all.

Everyone yelled dogscrimination is rampant

Dogscrimination

across our nation. They sang and danced along the way to the party.

Mr. Boots said hey we're almost there.

Laramie didn't say anything but they were headed in the vicinity of her home. She was relieved when they veered onto a street a couple of blocks from there. She definitely didn't want her humans to see her.

They finally arrived at the Siam Feral Compound which was next to the water tower. It was called that because the Siamese Feral Colony lived there. This week's party was happening there.

Mr. Boots said we have weekly parties at the compounds of different colonies.

BB said with all due respect Mr. Boots, if you get along, why are there porcupine bouncers?

It's merely precautionary. Wolves, coyotes and bobcats are welcome but occasionally they throw their weight around. The porcupines rapidly maintain order.

The Blue Russian Colony Compound live behind Alejandro's Authentic Italian Cafe'. It was their turn to bring the snacks. They brought delicious Italian cuisine including pizza, garlic knots, spaghetti, linguine, ravioli and lasagna. They didn't have to bring drinks since there was a natural spring in close proximity to the Siam Feral Compound.

The Tuxedo Colony was already there. They were helping build a fire.

The Persian Colony brought marshmallows to roast. They didn't bring sticks as there were various sizes of sticks in the woods.

The Maine Coon Colony was setting up the stage. They also wired the sound for the musicians.

Hal, the barred owl, was the editor-in-chief of "The Critter Town Criar". He was friends with

The Himalayan Colony. He had given them a copy of the most recent edition and they brought it to the party.

The local red ant colony arrived with portable picnic tables. They set up their tables under shiitake mushrooms. The ants were busily placing black and white checkered table cloths on the tables. They had coordinating placemats, napkins, plates and cups in preparation for the potluck dinner they had planned. Of course their potluck would consist of everything they could muster off of the Italian buffet.

The Manx Colony brought trash bags to clean up after the party. They even brought containers for the recyclable rubbish. They had also posted signs:

Skunks Welcome – Spraying Prohibited
No Littering
Now Entering A No Bully Zone

Jafra

Treat Animals Humanely Coalition (TAHC pronounced "tack") showed up for the party. TAHC membership was open to any animal interested in joining. TAHC members include dogs, cats, birds, raccoons, rabbits, woodchucks, chipmunks, porcupines and any other creature imaginable. Written on the banner fronting their table:

"You Can Tell A Lot About A Society By The Way It Treats Its Animals"
Gandhi

They set up a table with bumper stickers for the attendees to pick up and put on humans' cars. It was propaganda encouraging boycotting marine mammal parks and circuses that have performing animals. There were various stickers:

Orcas Are Dying To Entertain You

Dogscrimination

Leave Dolphin Pods Intact

Free Sibuyan the Captive Orca

Whales and Dolphins Don't Thrive In Tanks

Elephants Don't Enjoy Being Chained

The Circus Is Not Fun For the Animals

Don't Attend Circuses That Use Animals

Baby Elephants Need Their Mothers

Tigers Don't Enjoy Jumping Through Rings of Fire

Jafra

Dogscrimination

Chapter Eight

Get the Party Started

Laramie was amazed how organized the feral party was. Every colony had their own project and each member had his own task. It was dusk and the party was just about to get underway.

Laramie turned around to see an array of colors. There were such incredibly captivating colors gliding through the sky and descending toward the compound. She saw orange and black; dark maroon and cream; striking brown, red and black; metallic blue and grey; blue and silver; iridescent blue and red spots; black and white; yellow and black; blue, black and white. It was butterflies flying into the compound! The colors she viewed were that of monarchs, viceroys, mourning cloaks, red admirals, American lady butterflies, painted lady, tawny emperors, silver spotted skippers, wild indigo dusky wings, spring azures, eastern tailed blues, red-spotted purples, black swallowtails, zebra swallowtails, giant swallowtails, spicebush swallowtails and so many others. It was surreal watching all of the enchanting butterflies flying in. She noticed all the butterflies were flickering. As they grew closer, she discovered each butterfly was giving a firefly a ride and they were singing "Diamonds (In The Sky)" by Rihanna.

Laramie said everybody look to the sky. The butterflies are giving the fireflies a ride!

All were murmuring, enthralling, ohhhh, lovely, how pretty, magical, sensational and magnificent. Mr. Boots said the fireflies are part of the show. They flash in sequence to the all of the music. They have to conserve their energy for the party so the butterflies traditionally give them a ride. There were all types of instruments set up on the stage including woodwind, brass, percussion, string section, hurdy-gurdies and more. Various creatures entered from stage right. Trey turtle was the drummer. He was wearing a purple baseball cap sideways and had a Foo Fighters t shirt on. Rochelle raccoon was on bass and she had on tuxedo tails and white gloves with the fingertips of them clipped off. Kandy Kane, the naked mole rat, played the piano. The only thing she was wearing was a bob-styled wig in a hideous shade of fiery red which only put more emphasis on her big snout and her grey teeth. AJ, the skunk, was strumming his banjo. He was wearing a cowboy hat and a bolero tie. All of the other musicians were back stage awaiting their chance to perform.

Leon, a bald eagle, alighted on stage.

The squirrels living in the hollow of the poplar tree extended The American Flag.

Leon placed his right wing over his heart to lead the crowd in:

"I pledge allegiance to the flag of the United States of America, and to the republic for which it stands, one nation under God, indivisible, with liberty and justice for all."

The emcee, Mr. Boots, thanked Leon. He said please stand, feel free to sing along and he sang "The Star-Spangled Banner" by Francis Scott Key:

Oh, say can you see, by the dawn's early light
What so proudly we hailed at the twilight's last
gleaming?
Whose broad stripes and bright stars thro' the
perilous fight,
O'er the ramparts we watched were so gallantly
streaming.
And the rocket's red glare, the bombs bursting in air,
Gave proof thro' the night that our flag was still
there.
Oh, say does that Star - Spangled Banner yet wave
O'er the land of the free and the home of the brave.

The masses clapped and cheered.

Mr. Boots said here to get this party started, it's Silver Sam and The Blue Notes.

The singer was Silver Sam, a grey tabby wearing sunglasses, a black dinner jacket and a red fedora with a black feather. The Blue Notes were his cousins and they all wore steel blue dinner jackets.

Silver Sam said one, two, three and The Blue Notes began playing their instruments and singing "The Stray Cat Strut" by Stray Cats.

The crowd went wild while dancing and singing along.

When the song ended, Silver Sam asked if anyone would like to sing.

Laramie asked if they knew the music for "Fergalicious" by Fergie.

Silver Sam said yes.

Laramie jumped up on stage.

Silver Sam sang the intro...

Four, tres, two, uno Listen up y'all cause this is it,

the beat that I'm barkin' is de-li-cious

Then Laramie started singing *Laramielicious* to the
tune of "Fergalicious" by Fergie:

Laramielicious definition

Make them dogs go loco

they want to eat my bones and treats

I ordered them from SoHo

You can see me, you can't squeeze me

Ain't got fleas, I ain't fleazy

I got reasons why I tease 'em

Dogs just come and go like seasons

Laramielicious

(So delicious)

But I ain't ambiguous

And if you was suspicious

All that poop is fictitious

Jafra

I blow kisses

(Mwah)

That makes them dogs go bark, bark

And they be linin' down the block

Just to watch what I got

Silver Sam chimed in (Four, tres, two, uno)

So delicious

(I bark, bark)

So delicious

(I make them dogs go bark, bark)

So delicious

(They want a taste of what I got)

I'm Laramielicious

(T-t-tasty, tasty)

Laramielicious def-

Laramielicious def-

Laramielicious def-

Laramielicious definition

Make them dogs go crazy

Dogscrimination

They always claim they know me

Comin' to me call me baby

(Hey baby)

I'm the LA to the R, A, M, the I, the E

and can't no other doggy put it down like me

I'm Laramielicious

(So delicious)

My body stay'n vicious

I be at the dog park

Just workin' on my fitness

He's my witness

(Ooh wee) I make yo' dog go bark, bark

And he be runnin' down the block

Just to watch what I got

Silver Sam chimed in (Four, tres, two, uno)

So delicious

(I bark)

So delicious

(I make them dogs go bark, bark)

Jafra

So delicious

(They want a taste of what I got)

I'm Laramielicious

Laramie blew the crowd a kiss, **mwah** and curtsied.

Creatures were cat calling, whistling and applauding.

Silver Sam and The Blue Notes took a bow and exited stage left.

Mr. Boots was clapping while walking back on stage and said Laramie is quite the bohemian diva!

Hal, the barred owl, flew up in the pine tree closest to the stage. He announced himself with who, who, who, who cooks for you.

Everyone said hooray, Hal's here!

He read the advertisement for Squirrely Johnson's Handyman Business:

Unfortunately, the global economic crash, the worst since the Great Depression, has created a crisis in the Bird House Real Estate Market. Numerous birds have lost their homes as a result of the recession, high unemployment and subprime mortgages. Squirrely Johnson's Handyman Business's staff includes squirrels from his family, a variety of woodpecker species and woodchucks. Squirrely Johnson's Handyman Business provides free estimates for renovating any type of bird house for a new use. Squirrely Johnson's Handyman Business has experience in renovating blue bird houses, purple martin houses and more! Call today for a free estimate.

Jafra

The Harajuku ensemble included Burmese, Siamese and Malayan feral females. They were all dressed the same. They each had a tiny top hat with a wide fuchsia band; black and white striped arm warmers; a black velvet dress with a pink satin sash; a clownish skull embroidered on the skirt of the dress; shiny purple knickers with yellow bows at the knees; teal tights; hot pink and white striped leg warmers; and black ankle booties. They looked like they had just flown in from Shibuya, Tokyo, Japan. They got on stage. Choko, the lead singer, said we just found out that "Hello Kitty" is not a cat! What a drag!

The crowd mumbled bummer, no way, far out, unbelievable.

Then the music started, they sang "Harajuku Girls" by Gwen Stefani.

Once the Harajuku Girls left the stage, a dainty amber and brown tabby cat, Kiki, along with her sidekick, Hammie the hamster, walked on stage. (Kiki and Hammie were inseparable and although the general consensus was they were an odd pair, everyone accepted them as they were.) Kiki read an article from "The Critter Town Criar":

Neighborhood Birds Attack Cat

Earl, old man Holt's big orange tabby, got more than he bargained for Friday afternoon. He saw robins flying back and forth to the tallest magnolia in his yard. Earl scaled the tree to establish what fascination was enticing the robins. The mother robin saw him and alerted the entire neighborhood. Neighboring crows, blue jays, cardinals and mockingbirds began swooping down on Earl and pecking at him until he was out of the tree. Earl fled the scene. Reporter Odell, the chipmunk, was told by the authorities that no charges would be filed against the birds as it was clear the birds were defending the robins' nest. The robins have declined to press charges if, in future, Earl abides the "No Trespassing" sign posted on their nest's limb.

Someone was saying me next, me next. Finally they looked up and it was Evey, a young opossum, hanging by his tail wrapped around a limb. It thrilled him to sing. By his tail, he swung around the limb and jumped on stage. Good evening! I've made up lyrics to the tune "Jeremy" by Pearl Jam:

At home, gnawing sticks of ice cream pops,

With fudge on top, nothing was more fun, tail

wagged to a beat

And the cat strayed in to meow

Feline didn't give attention, oh

And the dog was something that feline wouldn't fear

Queen Laramie, the sticks, oh, ruled her world

Laramie barked at cats today

Laramie barked at cats today

Clearly I remember pickin' on the dog, seemed a

harmless little dog

Ooh, but we unleashed a lion, yeah

Gnashed her teeth and bit the fudge stick in jest

How could I forget?

And she hit me with the fudge sickle stick

My head hurtin', ooh, she'd bopped it so hard

Just like to say, oh, like to say I was hurt

Feline didn't give affection,

And the dog to the fact that feline didn't care

Queen Laramie, the sticks, oh ruled her world

Jafra

Laramie barked at cats today

Laramie barked at cats today

Laramie barked at barked at cats today

The crowd cheered as Evey took a bow.

Ringo said Ruby, Ruby, Ruby!

She gracefully entered from stage right. I've existed in predominate isolation and she sang "Numb" by Linkin Park. After the applause ended, a voice from the audience called for Ruby to tell a story. She said I fabricated stories to survive my cumbersome solitude and proceeded to tell a story:

A Home For Desi Duck

A pet store had ducklings for sale that were only 24 hours old and Cherise bought one. She named him Desi duck. Cherise was the first being her duck saw once out of the box. She learned that the first creature the duckling sees is presumed its mother which is imprinting. Desi thought Cherise was his mom. Every time she went out of his sight he made a distressed chirping noise. She kept him until he was full grown and decided he should live at the lake. Cherise enlisted her friends Dabney, Mobley and Dier to accompany Desi duck and her to the park. Dabney drove and Desi duck was in a box beside Cherise. They had a nice picnic before releasing Desi duck. She put him out in the water, said bye and returned to the picnic table. A few minutes later, she saw a little boy carrying her duck. She took Desi duck from him and explained he was her duck. She took Desi duck back to the water. A photographer saw her and explained that hand-raised ducks will

Jafra

not survive in the wild. She decided she would have to find an alternate home for Desi duck and put him back in his box. As they were leaving the park, they were pulled over by a park ranger. He came to the driver's window, smirking while stating, you have been reported as having stolen a duck. Dabney replied, no sir, this is the duck we came with. Cherise opened the box and Desi duck popped his head out of the box. Cherise explained the scenario. The park ranger said domestic ducks aren't permitted at the park and he let them go on their way. She went to Rusty Wheelbarrow, a farming supply store, to buy Desi duck some food. She told the clerk about her predicament. He proceeded to tell her that he had a farm with a pond and Desi duck could live there. Cherise said if you promise you won't eat Desi duck, that would be ideal. The clerk promised. And so it was, Desi duck moved to the pond on the farm. He was in awe to make the acquaintance of other animals who lived on the farm. Fortuna was on Desi duck's side. It was there he encountered the love of his life and his best friend, a black swan named Jasmine.

The audience clapped and called out encore, encore.

Mr. Boots asked if Ruby would grant the crowd another story.

Ruby bowed and began telling:

Cotton Tales - A Bunny Folklore

Zsazu had just given birth to four precious bunnies. She had wisely chosen a safe place for her nest and they were carefully covered with grass to camouflage them. At the break of day, she left her babies to eat breakfast. She knew of a robust field of clover across the street. As she leapt onto the street, she was struck by a vehicle. The driver was texting and never fathomed a life had been taken or that four other lives were now in grave danger as a result of the reckless decision to text while driving. The four babies waited all day and night for their loving mother's return, to no avail. At dawn, the first born told his bunny siblings he would set out to search for their mom. He climbed out of the burrow into the dew-soaked grass. He was so frail from lack of nutrition, he could not go any further. Ron Anderson was working in his yard and came across the bunny. He peaked under the grass to find the three other bunnies. He called his wife, Joyce, to tell her about this. Joyce left her office and went to a local pet store to pick up necessary paraphernalia to take care of the bunnies. When Joyce arrived home, she made a crib out of a box for the baby bunnies, placed them in the crib and took them inside. Every time Joyce touched any of the bunnies, she would softly call them baby. Joyce lovingly picked up a bunny, said hi baby, fed it and then another until all four had been fed. It was bed time but Joyce wanted to check on the babies. Sadly, the gallant bunny who trekked off to save his family had perished. Ron and she were somber as well were the siblings of the bunny. Wisely, however, Joyce decided to weigh each bunny. Then, she weighed each bunny morning and night to ascertain they were gaining weight. The bunnies grew and the time had come to release them. Ron and Joyce set them free in a celebratory way. Ever since then, bunny folklore is when a human says "hi baby" to any bunny, the bunny knows it is safe.

Ruby was given a standing ovation.

Lars was an Afghan hound who had witnessed his humans posting photos of him on Craigslist. Underneath the photos, their posting stated:

We had no clue Afghan hounds grew to be so big. He takes up too much room in our house and eats too much. Besides, we're pregnant so he has to go. We are charging a $500.00 rehoming fee to ensure he goes to a good home. Do not flag this message.

Dogscrimination

In the depths of his despair he ran away from home. He was ultimately arrested by the critter cop but escaped the animal shelter the night before his execution. He affiliated himself with a pack of wolves and changed his name to Pup Bark. He showed up with his clique. He was wearing a black dew rag with white skulls, a black leather vest with "Wandering Wolves" embroidered on the back, and chaps. His fur was long and styled in dread locks. He ran onto the stage and started singing to the tune of "Bawitdaba" by Kid Rock:

Barktodbark da bone a bone a dig diggit diggit said
the doogy said sit & stay doogy
Barktodbark da bone a bone a dig diggit diggit said
the doogy said sit & stay doogy
Barktodbark da bone a bone a dig diggit diggit said
the doogy said sit & stay doogy

Jafra

Barktodbark da bone a bone a dig diggit diggit said

the doogy said sit & stay doogy

My name puuuuuuuuuuuuuuuuup... Pup Bark

Barktodbark da bone a bone a dig diggit diggit said

the doogy said sit & stay doogy

Barktodbark da bone a bone a dig diggit diggit said

the doogy said sit & stay doogy

And this is for the perils felt by the ferals

The daytime sleepers and nighttime creepers

Where the homeless roam and the dog without a bone

The human freaks, the nerds and the geeks

Barktodbark da bone a bone a dig diggit diggit said

the doogy said sit & stay doogy

Pup Bark dove off the stage into his clique. He and his clique were moshing.

Mr. Boots sternly spoke into the microphone and said Wandering Wolves must immediately cease their rambunctious capers.

Dogscrimination

They capitulated. They ate some of the Italian cuisine. They listened as Asia, the bobcat, read a poem Claude, a yellow swallowtail butterfly, had submitted to "The Critter Town Criar":

<u>My Second Chance</u>

Fearing for my life in an unseasonable cold
Caring hands lifted me into their fold
Placed in the warmth and now quite secure
My future suddenly seemed somewhat obscure
Two days and nights would surreally go by
My guardian sweetly nursed me, this butterfly
I suddenly felt the warmth of the sun
My guardian knew the time had come
That I return to my kingdom
After takeoff, I flew around in sort of a dance
To the one who gave me my second chance

Mr. Boots thanked Asia.

The crowd wept tears of joy.

Jafra

One unusually cold day in April, Liezel Rhea Lester saved Claude on her walk home from school. His poem was his grateful tribute to her. Willie asked Silver Sam if he could borrow a guitar.

Sure thing Willie.

He entered stage right and said I wrote "A Dog Named Ned" about an old friend of mine. He started picking and singing:

> *Let me tell ya 'bout a dog named Ned*
> *He's real nice unless he ain't been fed*
> *Then you're really better off dead*
> *Round the hungry dog named Ned*
>
> *Ned's a brindle colored rescue dog*
> *When he's hungry he eats like a hog*
> *Then goes out for a mile long jog*
> *After that home to sleep like a log*

Ned's gotta boxer friend named Mike

They often go out for a nice hike

But sometimes Mike rides his bike

Many say the dogs look alike

Ned's gotta temper that's hot red

That temper never ever helps Ned

Ned should really lose his short fuse

Instead Ned continues to use

Ned had a home but he had to bale

His humans left him at the foreclosure sale

Ned's lookin' for a permanent home

But for now Ned still has to roam

There's lotsa dogs just like Ned

Ain't got no home ain't got no bed

Many of 'em think they're better off dead

Just like the ones around hungry Ned

Jafra

Willie took a bow as all applauded.

Sean from The Maine Coon Colony read from "The Critter Town Criar":

<u>Atkins Family Seed Kitchen</u>

The Atkins Family have made changes to their annual Atkins Family Seed Kitchen. In addition to the neighborhood birds, squirrels are now welcome to dine at the Atkins Family Seed Kitchen. According to reporter Katie, the grey fox, last year Ms. Atkins had chased off the squirrel on a daily basis. One day he didn't show up and she became concerned that she had broken the little squirrel's spirit. They concurred that squirrels need to eat too so they revised the kitchen rules this year. Ms. Atkins said it has been a great

success and there has been plenty of
food to go around.

Mr. Boots exclaimed hey, let's all sing "Atomic
Dog" by George Clinton in honor of the
protesters. Silver Sam and The Blue Notes started
playing. The crowd began singing and dancing.
They were clapping, cheering and laughing at the
end of the song.

Laramie was so happy and having such a good
time but was also learning so many new things.

Mia from The Manx Colony read an
announcement from "The Critter Town Criar":

Feral Fixin' Scheduled

The quarterly Feral Fixin' is scheduled
for this coming Saturday, weather
permitting. The Feral Friends Society
will be picking up all ferals interested in
being spayed or neutered. This is also

a good opportunity to get your three-year rabies shot too.

Mr. Boots said thank you for the public service announcement Mia. If you've already been spade or neutered but it's time for your three-year rabies shot, we urge you to do so. I encourage all of you ferals out there to do the responsible thing and get neutered or spayed. We ferals have a dream which is to put an end to homeless cats. The humans certainly aren't succeeding at that.

The crowd gleefully agreed.

Zephyr jumped on stage styling a tan zoot suit with black and white pinstripes; and a tan fedora with a black band around it. I dedicate "Bully" by Shinedown to Portia and he began to sing.

Mr. Boots shook Zephyr's paw and said good job. We all need to take a stand against bullies.

The crowd clapped and gave him a standing ovation.

Zona, the mourning dove, alighted on stage to read:

Bird Summit Reviews Voyeurism Accusations

Neighborhood birds proclaimed Dr. Piper is a voyeur. The birds complained he gapes at them with binoculars while they bathe, eat, nest, feed their nestlings and teach their young to fly. He is also frequently taking photographs of all species of birds. After copious complaints, a bird summit was conducted to evaluate the assertions against Dr. Piper. Following a thorough investigation of the allegations, the bird summit concluded Dr. Piper is not a voyeur but an ornithologist. He is absolutely no threat to the neighborhood birds. The summit added all birds should be grateful that some humans still marvel and appreciate their beauty.

KD was a mammoth-sized wild boar. The preferred analogy is KD is to the average boar as a killer whale to a goldfish. All of the other wild boars made fun of her because she was morbidly obese. She blamed her weight problem on defective genetics but it was common knowledge she was a gourmand.

She had been backstage during the entire party with the mink sisters, Greta and Pheenie. Greta and Pheenie had the daunting task of attempting to get her all dolled up. Greta put false eyelashes on KD while Pheenie teased a blonde wig. Once her makeup was complete, they put the wig on her and wrapped a hot pink boa around her neck.

Greta and Pheenie were the backup singers to KD and they entered stage left. KD strutted onto the stage. Someone yelled what's shakin' bacon. Although it was a discourteous heckling, the audience roared with laughter. She started swinging her hips and singing "All About That Bass" by Meghan Trainor.

The audience applauded KD as she took a bow. Disastrously, she lost her footing and fell off the stage. Fortunately, she did not fall on anyone. (What a catastrophe that would have been!) Most all were in tears they were laughing so hard at the clumsy gargantuan of a boar. In true form, KD stopped by the buffet and took enough to feed an army. Everyone knew it was all for herself.

In an attempt to reroute the crowd's attention, Mr. Boots walked on stage while clapping and thanking KD and the minks. We have breaking news in the neighborhood. The Leinart family has adopted a German shepherd named Jjax who is a war hero. Jjax has an impressive resume. He was born at Lackland Air Force Base in Texas. After training, he went with Army Staff Sargent Lem Atchley to Kandahar, Afghanistan. He spent two successful years finding Improvised Explosive Devices (IEDs). His last discovery of IEDs saved hundreds of innocent women and children as well as his entire unit. He received a Medal of Honor and returned to the United States to live with the Leinart family. We're proud to welcome Jjax to our community and hope to have him attend at our next fiesta. Now we will hear from Benia.

Benia, the red shoulder hawk, flew on stage to read:

Drones Concern Bird Community

The use of drones is an increasingly growing concern in the bird community. The general consensus is drones will lead to crashes, drive up the cost of collision insurance and cause unnecessary injuries or casualties. During the bird summit, it was agreed that more bird traffic controllers must be trained and put in force to minimize these potential risks. Anyone interested in applying may pick up an application at the "The Critter Town Criar" office. All applicants will be subject to a background check, must have a clean flying record and pass a drug screening. Remember to inform the recruiter if you've recently consumed poppy seeds as that will show up on your drug screening.

Jafra

Mr. Boots thanked Benia as she flew off stage.

Nub Atkins was the newest reporter for "The Critter Town Criar". He was a silver Siamese/tabby mix who had lost his right back paw in a car accident. He used crutches to assist him to get on stage and then read:

Windstorm Destroys Ant Hills

Hundreds of black ant hills were destroyed on Saturday. The windstorm was not weather related, however. A little girl in the neighborhood, Ellie, was playing with the leaf blower she had given her dad for Father's Day. The authorities discussed the incident with her and she was unaware she had disrupted the ant hills. She explained she merely enjoyed blowing leaves, twigs and the occasional plastic bag from Z Mart. She did not intend to

Dogscrimination

disrupt the ant hills or inflict harm on anyone. No fines will be assessed but Ellie has been ordered to attend a safety seminar on the proper use of leaf blowers.

Mr. Boots thanked Nub as he walked off stage. Suddenly, River, a pileated woodpecker, flew onto stage. He said, I have received a devastating tweet I must relay. Just in from the Republic of Zimbabwe, Africa. Cecil, a beloved thirteen year old Southwest African lion, who lived in Hwange National Park in Matabeleland North, Zimbabwe, was lured out from the sanctuary of the park. He was shot and killed by a hunter from the United States of America. The hunter was described as a trophy hunter and is allegedly responsible for poaching other beautiful creatures.

The crowd began burbling.

Mr. Boots returned to the stage and said let's pause for a moment of silence in memory of Cecil. Traveler the Border collie, who attended Cheng Ping Ren's party, entered from stage right. He said many humans are greedy, self-centered and treat everything in the world as if they own it. Those humans should pay close attention to us. They would learn to respect all living creatures, promote harmony and enjoy the beauty in each day. He sang "Imagine" by John Lennon.

The crowd gave him a standing ovation.

Asa, the woodchuck, walked on stage to read a public service announcement from TAHC:

Local Water Sprinklers

Upcoming summer months may bring periods of drought. Many birds have difficulty locating water for hydration and personal hygiene. Local water sprinklers can be located in the nursery departments at most big box retailers. Birds are urged to frequent these stores during the dry season.

Mr. Boots thanked Asa. He said I will read one more story from the "The Critter Town Criar" before intermission:

Lizards Beware

Lizards in the Shady Grove community should beware of 1015 Sundown Lane. The humans who reside there do not tolerate lizards in their home. The lady of the house, who asked to remain anonymous, stated that any lizard found scurrying inside their home would be promptly vacuumed with a shop vac. We do release the lizards but simply do not want them in our home. Mr. Speedster, head of a lizard family recently shop vacuumed out of this home, countered, on the surface it may seem humane but in reality it disbands lizard families because they are neither captured together nor released in the same vicinity.

Mr. Boots said yikes, that must be the strangest trip any lizard has ever taken. I would stay away from that place altogether if I were a lizard. Let's take a brief intermission now.

Chapter Nine

Reality Sets In

Psst, psst, said Ruby to get BB's attention. He walked over and asked what she needed.

I found this article from "The Critter Town Criar" and it is about Laramie. There's even a picture of her included in it.

What?

Jafra

Yes, her family is looking for her! She handed it to him.

He read it and said I don't want to show this to Laramie until we've had a chance to discuss this. Let's round up the protestors.

All the protestors gathered around and BB read the article:

<u>Babelay Dog Missing – Parents Distraught</u>

On Sunday afternoon, the Babelay family notified the authorities that their dog was missing. Officer Justin Case was interviewed by Arthur, the great horned owl, of the "The Critter Town Criar". He told Arthur the Babelays were distraught and believed someone had stolen their beautiful Bichon Frise', Laramie. Ms. Babelay told the officer they came home from the movies to find her gone. She said the only other

Dogscrimination

stop they made was at Pets-R-A-Big Deal. She said they couldn't have been away from home for more than three hours. They hold out every hope she will be returned to them safe and sound. She was last seen wearing a red bandana that had white bones outlined in purple on it. She is micro chipped. If you have any information about the whereabouts of Laramie you are asked to contact the authorities immediately.

They were all so confused and not sure what to think.

About that time, Laramie bounced up. Hi gang!

All of the dogs circled around her.

She sensed something was amiss.

BB said Laramie, there is an article in "The Critter Town Criar" about you.

What?

Yes, and among other things, it states your humans are *distraught* that you are missing. I thought your humans were cruel to you, yet you're not underweight, you're well groomed, your teeth are pearly white and you don't have fleas or ticks. Why *did* you run away from home? Because I'm dogscriminated against by them!

Discriminated how, Ruby cried.

They don't take me to restaurants, movies, grocery shopping and they frequently leave me home alone.

Ringo asked if they spent time with her when they were at home.

Of course they do! Heck, I have my own pillow in their bed. When either of 'em are sick, I stay by their side until they're better. They call me their "dogtor". My mom is funny too. Every time she picks me up she says "beep, beep, beep, beep, beep" like she's a machine moving a large piece of equipment. She'll say you're my sweetheart. Then we'll sing "Ho Hey" by The Lumineers. Ha, then we double high-five and hug. When she makes peanut butter sandwiches, she regularly puts a smidge on a treat for me. She says it doesn't matter how rich you are, life doesn't get any better than this. She'll take me for a walk in the morning and a couple of times in the afternoon. I get to ride to the recycle center with her. When I ride to the bank with her, the teller customarily gives me a bone. When I ...

Willie interrupted and sternly said that sounds like paradise little girl.

They all started talking concurrently and pushing her.

You don't get beaten, you have plenty of food, water and love.

Your life seems like heaven on earth, girlfriend. Utopia, yeah.

You don't have to work at a job you hate, man.

They don't ignore you. I'll bet your humans even take you to the dog park.

You don't have an awful sister who steals your food, bullies you, humiliates you in front of your friends and tears up your toys.

Mr. Boots hissed and brashly stated I'll bet your humans bag your poop like it's gold.

She started crying as they closed in on her, questioning her and pushing her.

Laramie.

Laramie.

Laramie!

Humph, wh, what, she looked up. It was her mom gently patting her to awaken her.

Laramie, you're having a dream. Your dad and I just got home. We picked up this stuffed raccoon for you from Pets-R-A-Big Deal. She picked her

Dogscrimination

up and hugged her while saying I love you Laramie. You make life worth living.

Laramie snuggled in her mom's arms. Her dream had opened her eyes to the realization that life is remarkably hard for many animals in the world. Regardless of the species, many creatures are dogscriminated. Although dogscrimination is rampant across our nation (and the world), she realized she's a fortunate dog. She thought *I make life worth living, that's a big job for a little dog!* The song "Wake Me Up" by Aloe Blacc began playing.

Acknowledgements

Armstrong, Louis. "Jeepers Creepers." Blueberry Hill. Milan Records, 1962.

Arnold, Malcolm. Theme on "The Bridge on the River Kwai" soundtrack. Legacy/Columbia, 1963.

The Beatles. "Yesterday." Help! Parlophone, 1965.

Blacc, Aloe. "Wake Me Up." EP. Aloe Blacc Recording, Inc., 2013.

Cecil. Male African lion senselessly killed July 1, 2015 in Zimbabwe.

Clinton, George. "Atomic Dog." Computer Games. Capitol, 1982.

Cowperthwaite, Gabriela; Despres, Eli; Zimmerman, Tim. "Blackfish." CNN Films and Manny O. Productions. Magnolia Pictures, 2013.

Craigslist. Newmark, Craig. Classified Advertisements, 1995.

Crow, Sheryl. "All I Wanna Do." Tuesday Music Club. A & M, 1993.

Dodd, Jimmie. "The Mickey Mouse Club March."

The Eagles. "Hotel California." Hotel California. Asylum, 1976.

Fergie. "Fergalicious." The Dutchess. A & M – Interscope, 2006.

Foo Fighters. American Rock Band.

Gandhi, Mahatma. Anti-War Activist.

Helms, Bobby. "Jingle Bell Rock." Decca, 1957.

Jackson, Michael. "Thriller." Thriller. Epic, 1982.

Key, Francis Scott. "The Star-Spangled Banner." 1814.

Kid Rock. "Jeremy." Devil Without a Cause. Atlantic, 1999.

Lambert, Miranda. "Mama's Broken Heart." Four the Record. RCA Nashville, 2011.

Lennon, John. "Imagine". Parlophone Catalogue, 1971.

Linkin Park. "Numb". Don Gilmore, Linkin Park. Warner Bros. 2003.

The Lumineers. "Ho Hey." The Lumineers. Dualtone, 2012.

Macy's Parade. 1924 to date.

McCartney, Paul. "Great Day." Flaming Pie. Capitol, 1992.

Nelson, Willie. "On the Road Again." Honeysuckle Rose. Columbia, 1979.

Norman, Monty. "James Bond Theme." "Dr. No" soundtrack. United Artists, 1962.

Pearl Jam. "Jeremy." Ten. Epic/Legacy, 1992.

Rihanna. "Diamonds (In The Sky)".

Unapologetic. Def Jam Records, 2012.

Roosevelt, Eleanor. First Lady of the United States 1933 – 1945.

Sam and the Womp. "Bom Bom." Bom Bom. Big Beat Records/Atlantic, 2012.

Sandburg, Carl. American Poet.

Shinedown. "Bully." Amaryllis. Atlantic, 2012.

Stefani, Gwen. "Harajuku Girls." Love. Angel. Music. Baby. Interscope Records, 2004.

Stray Cats. "Stray Cat Strut." Built For Speed. EMI/EMI Records (USA), 1982.

The Talking Heads. "This Must Be the Place." Speaking in Tongues. Rhino/Warner Bros., 1983.

Tebow, Tim. American Football.

Traditional. "Row, Row, Row Your Boat." 1852.

Trainor, Meghan. "All About That Bass." Title. Epic, 2015.

Tweet. Dorsey, Jack; Williams, Evan; Stone, Biz; Glass, Noah. Message on Twitter, an online social networking service. 2006.

About the Author

Jafra loves all animals and has been fortunate to enjoy friendships with a variety of animals throughout her lifetime. She currently lives in Knoxville, Tennessee with her husband and their Bichon Frise'.

Made in the USA
Columbia, SC
15 June 2022

61728881R00102